MONSTERS, MONSTERS!

By Michaela Muntean
Illustrated by Richard Walz

A SESAME STREET/GOLDEN PRESS BOOK

Published by Western Publishing Company, Inc.
in conjunction with Children's Television Workshop.

© 1992, 1987 Children's Television Workshop. Sesame Street puppet characters © 1992 Jim Henson Productions, Inc. All rights reserved. Printed in the U.S.A. No part of this book may be reproduced or copied in any form without written permission from the publisher. SESAME STREET®, the SESAME STREET SIGN®, and THE SESAME STREET BOOK CLUB are trademarks and service marks of Children's Television Workshop. All other trademarks are the property of Western Publishing Company, Inc. Library of Congress Catalog Card Number: 86-82358 ISBN: 0-307-24161-0

Baby Monsters

Baby monsters are just like other babies. They need lots of love and care.

Monster mommies sing monster lullabies to their babies. Monster daddies take their babies for walks in the park.

Baby monsters have many things to learn before they become grown-up monsters.

"Chew everything carefully," mommy monsters say.

Little monsters like to play with their food before they eat it, but they always leave their places clean by eating their cups and plates.

Little monsters must learn to keep their fur neat and tidy. "Remember to comb your elbows and behind your knees," daddy monsters say.

Some monsters like to look scary, so they go to scary-face classes. Today the teacher is showing the little monsters how to make a monster frown.

"Be careful not to scare yourselves," the monster teacher reminds them.

No matter how big or strong or furry or scary-looking little monsters grow up to be, they always remember their monster manners.

"Excuse me, sir," Herry says every time he bumps into someone.

And little monsters never forget to give monster-size hugs to the monsters they love.

Monster Nursery Rhymes

Old King Cookie was a merry old soul,
and a merry old soul was he.
He called for his pie, and he called for his cake,
and he called for his cookie jars three!

Oscar, Oscar, quite contrary,
how does your garden grow?
With sardine cans and old tin pans
and spider webs all in a row!

Herry had a little lamb
whose fur was monster-blue.
Wherever Herry Monster went
the monster lamb went, too.

Hey, diddle, diddle,
one cat's got a fiddle,
and a monster jumped over the moon.
A little dude laughed,
for it's so out of sight—
this party could go on till noon!

LOCH NESS
MONSTER

ROTTEN
APPLE
GALLERY

ABOMINABLE
SNOW MONSTER

FRANKENSTEIN
MONSTER

The Monster Hall of Fame

As the Mayor of Monsters, I welcome you to the Monster Hall of Fame. Throughout history, we monsters have taken monster-size steps in every field from science to sports.

Sadly, we have also had our share of rotten apples. Yes, even monsters sometimes do beastly things!

You have probably heard of our distant cousins the Loch Ness Monster, the Abominable Snow Monster, and the Frankenstein Monster. These monsters, who stomp about and cause problems, give us respectable monsters a bad name.

Here we have another rotten example. This is Cookie the Terrible. He cleaned out every cookie jar in Europe before he was caught red-handed in Chocolate Square!

Let us move on to some finer examples of monsterdom.
I'm sure you have all heard of that great baseball player
Mickey Monster. He hit some monster-size home runs when
he played in the big leagues.

If you ever visit the Monsterpolitan Museum, you will see paintings by our greatest artist, Vincent van Monster. Here in the Hall of Fame, we are monstrously proud to have his self-portrait.

The great scientist Madame Furry will always be
remembered for her contributions to monsterkind.
    Please remember the Hall of Fame monsters we have
seen here today. Great thinkers. Great artists. Great
monsters, all. *They* are the ones who make me proud to call
myself a monster!

The Truth About Monsters

Hello, everybody! It is I, lovable, furry old
Grover Monster. Did you know that some people
have very silly ideas about monsters? Oh, it is true—
and it is terrible! That is why I am here to tell you
the *truth* about monsters.

First of all, many people think that monsters are big and ugly and scary.

Now, look at my friend Herry. It is true that he is big. It is true that he is not as cute and adorable as I am. But he is not scary. Are you, Herry?

Herry may not be a scary monster, but he is a scary ghost!

Many people think that monsters like to hide in closets and under beds at night. This is ridiculous.

Look at this closet. It is a mess. Would you like to stand in there with all that junk? I will show you how silly that would be.

I was right. That was silly.

Now, look under this bed. No monster with any sense
would hide under there because he would get dust balls in
his fur. Here, I will show you!

I, Grover Monster, was right again. Excuse me while I go
take a bath.

Hello, again. It is I, lovable, furry old *clean* Grover. I am back to tell you more truths about monsters.

Some people think that monsters like to hide behind bushes and then jump out and scare you. This is another silly idea. Look at this bush. Do you think there is a monster behind it?

Uh-oh. That big green bush said something. Oh, my goodness! It is not a bush. It is a big furry green monster! Please forgive my monstrous mistake.

The green bush, er…monster has asked me to stay and play with him. He is waiting for his mommy because he is not old enough to walk home alone.

So the next time someone tells you about monsters, you can say that you already know the *truth* about monsters!